Little Zel
and Friends

Caroline Castle & Sam Childs

Hutchinson

London Sydney Auckland Johannesburg

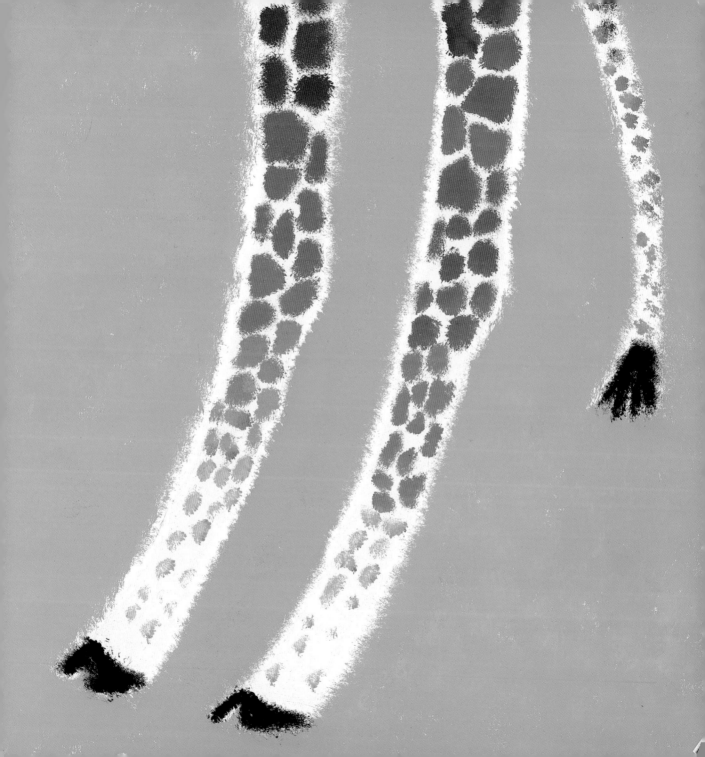

'Don't make me laugh,' said Giraffe.

'I'm too **toll,**

and you're too small.'

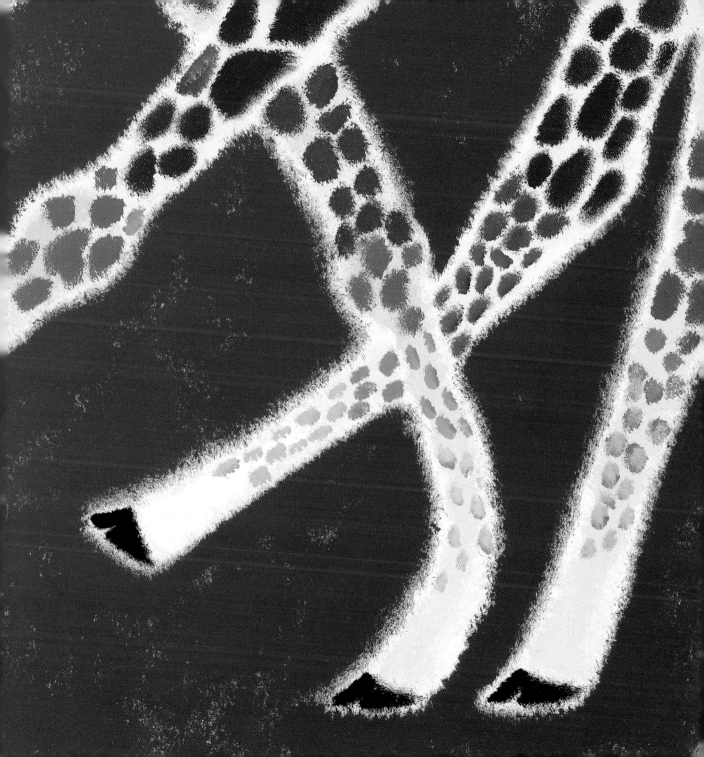

'Let's **race,**
funny face!'

'Oh, no,' said Hippo.

'You're too **fast,** and I'm too s l o w.'

'Wish I could,
but I can't...

...I'm too **heavy,'**

said Elephant.

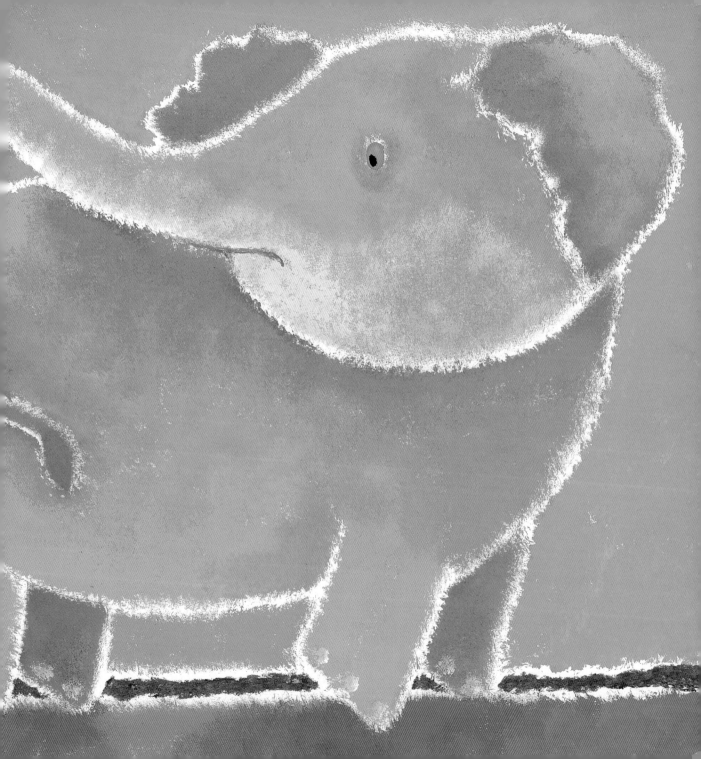

'Let's **hide!**'
'You fit just so,' said Rhino.

'But I'm too **wide** to slip inside.'

'Oh yes,' said Big Zeb.
'Snuggle down close to me.'

One **big,**

one small...